The Sleepover Club

The Sleepover Club
at Rosie's

THE PET SHOW

by Rose Impey

Collins
An imprint of HarperCollinsPublishers

First published in Great Britain by Collins in 1997
Collins is an imprint of HarperCollins *Publishers* Ltd
77-85 Fulham Palace Road, Hammersmith,
London, W6 8JB

7 9 8

Text copyright © Rose Impey 1997

ISBN 0 00 675235 7

Printed and bound in Great Britain by
Caledonian International Book Manufacturing Ltd,
Glasgow G64

Please come to a sleepover
at Rosie's

75 Welby Drive
Welby Avenue
Cuddington
Leicester

Please come at
6pm on Friday 6 December.
And bring your sleepover kit.

You will need to be collected
about 11am on Saturday because
of the Pet Show!

From Rosie Cartwright

SLEEPOVER KIT LIST

1. Sleeping bag
2. Pillow
3. Pyjamas or a nightdress
4. Slippers
5. Toothbrush, toothpaste, soap etc
6. Towel
7. Teddy
8. A creepy story
9. Food for a midnight feast: chocolate, crisps, sweets, biscuits. In fact, anything you like to eat.
10. A torch
11. Hairbrush
12. Hair things like a bobble or hairband, if you need them
13. Clean knickers and socks
14. Sleepover diary

CHAPTER ONE

Oh, hi there. You haven't seen my dog, Pepsi, have you? She's gone missing. She's a black spaniel. She's escaped lots of times before and someone always brings her back. The trouble is that this time she's in season and, if we don't find her soon, you know what *that* could mean. My mum's in a real razz with me! I didn't mean to leave the front gate open.

The thing is, last week I had this big argument with her and Dad because they won't let Pepsi have puppies. It's bad enough they won't let *me* have a brother or sister, now they won't let the dog have a baby either!

So Mum thinks I let Pepsi out on purpose. Dad'll go ballistic when he knows. It would have to happen just now, when I was in their good books for a change.

I know, why don't you come with me to look for Pepsi, then I can tell you about our latest Sleepover Club adventure? That was all to do with pets. It was excellent. Come on, we'll head for the park, that's one of Pepsi's favourite places, and I'll tell you all about it on the way.

It all started with the Pet Show in the Village Hall. It was organised to raise money for an animal refuge and the whole Sleepover Club decided to enter. We first heard about it at Brownies a few weeks ago. We all go to Brownies, everyone in the Sleepover Club, even Fliss and Lyndz who are old enough to go up to Guides if they want to, but they're waiting for the rest of us. We like to stick together. Can you remember who everyone is?

First there's Laura Mackenzie – we call her Kenny. She's my best friend.

Felicity Sidebotham – we call her Fliss. Oh boy, I'm glad I'm not called Sidebotham. She gets teased all the time.

Then there's Lyndsey Collins – we call her Lyndz. It was Lyndz that got us into trouble this time, or at least her dog, Buster, did. He's a menace.

And Rosie Cartwright. The sleepover was at Rosie's, which was totally cool because she's never let us stay at her place before and her house is perfect for sleepovers: big and old and a bit spooky.

That just leaves me – Francesca Theresa Thomas, but you can call me Frankie.

So, that's all of us. Yeah, yeah, I know five's not a good number, someone's bound to get left out, but five's how many there are, so that's that.

Now, back to the story. Brown Owl showed us some posters about the Pet Show and asked us each to take one home and put it up somewhere. She said she wanted all of us who have pets to go in for it as part of our Pet Lovers Badge. I couldn't wait to ask Mum and Dad if I could take Pepsi. I was sure I'd win, but then so were all the others. And the trouble was three of us have dogs. We started arguing straight away, as soon as Brown Owl had finished.

"Buster's so smart he's bound to win," said Lyndz. She's got this weird little Jack Russell terrier, he's absolutely mad. You should see him.

"Dream on," I said. "He's not that smart and he won't beat Pepsi. She's so cute."

"Well," said Rosie, "Jenny's smart *and* she's cute."

Which is true. Jenny's a mongrel, but she's got a lot of sheepdog in her. Her coat's really shiny, black and white and she's got a wonderful big tail. And she's clever, too. So that made me mad. But Fliss made me even madder.

"Well, you can't all win," she said, smiling.

"Oh, very good," I said. "Now tell us something we don't know."

"I might win," said Kenny.

Kenny doesn't have a dog, although she'd love one, but she's had loads of other pets. She had a hamster once, and a rabbit, but they both died. And a cat called Tinkerbell, which ran away, and a bird called Bobby which flew out of the window, and a goldfish, which the cat ate before she ran away. She's not had much luck so far.

Now she's got a big white rat called Merlin. She says he's mega-intelligent and she's training him, but he doesn't seem to have learnt much! There's something about the way Kenny lets him sit on her shoulder that gives me the heebie-jeebies.

Kenny's sister, Molly the Monster, shares a bedroom with Kenny and she hates rats, so Merlin has to live in the garage. I know Kenny's my best friend and everything but, to be honest, I agree with Molly; I wouldn't want to sleep in a room with a rat either.

The Pet Show wasn't only for dogs, of course, you could take other pets. On the poster it said there were prizes in each different class: hamsters, rabbits, cats, and lots of others, but there was no mention of rats!

"It's not fair," said Kenny. "What about Merlin?"

"Don't worry, Laura," said Brown Owl. "I'll find out if rats are allowed."

So that just left Fliss, who was a real problem, because Fliss doesn't have a pet at all, apart from her goldfish, Bubbles. And you can't do much with a goldfish, can you?

"It's just not fair," she said. "My mum's so mean."

Fliss's mum is not mean, she's just mega house-proud.

"You have loads of things we don't have," I reminded her. "You've got more clothes than a supermodel for a start."

"And toys…" said Lyndz.

"And CDs…" said Kenny.

"OK, OK, but I haven't got a pet to take to the Pet Show and you lot have."

Which was true and we couldn't seem to think of a way round it. Anyway, there was no point in us arguing about which one of us was going to win because we already knew who would. You didn't have to be a genius to work that out.

CHAPTER TWO

"The dreaded M&Ms," said Kenny. We all made being-sick noises.

It was lunchtime and we were sitting on the steps in the studio at school with just the spotlights on. We were supposed to be working on a dance routine for assembly but we were having a rest.

"Why would they win?" said Rosie. She's new to our school, so she doesn't know all about the M&Ms yet.

"Because they win everything," said Fliss.

Have I told you about the M&Ms?

They're in our class at school and, as if that isn't bad enough, they go to Brownies as well. Their real names are Emma Hughes and Emily Berryman, but we call them the M&Ms. Or sometimes The Queen and The Goblin. I'll tell you why:

Emma Hughes is tall and soppy and really annoying, but she's everybody's favourite: our teacher's, the headteacher's, the dinner ladies', Brown Owl's, Snowy Owl's... *And* all the boys like her. She always gets the best marks and gold stars and wins competitions like the Brownie Cook's Challenge and gets picked to be milk monitor and take the register. She is so stuck up. That's why we call her The Queen.

Emily Berryman's nearly as bad. She's dead small, with big eyes and a deep, gruff voice, so we call her The Goblin. She always gets good marks and wins things too. We don't know how they do it. We think it's because they cheat, but we haven't been able to prove it. Not yet, anyway.

The worst thing about them is the way they whisper and giggle. They are seriously gruesome. The moment Brown Owl told us about the Pet Show they started giggling and behaving as if they'd already won.

And the annoying thing is they probably will win. Emma Hughes has this dog that she's always bragging about and Emily Berryman has a cat. We've never seen them, but we've heard plenty about them.

The M&Ms are our worst enemies and the thing we hate most in the whole world, the whole universe in fact, is being beaten by them.

"We've got to think of a way to stop them," I said.

"How?" said Lyndz. "I don't think Pepsi and Buster stand much of a chance against Duchess of Drumshaw The Third and Sabrina Sprightly Dancing."

Can you believe those names? I didn't make them up. I don't suppose that's what they call them everyday, when they take them out for walks or call them for their food. That would be too stupid, even for them. But those are their pedigree names and when they're showing off that's what they call them.

"Pepsi's a pedigree spaniel," I said, "but she doesn't have a stupid name like that." She's the best dog in the world and I love her to bits. She's got a black curly coat and long ears that trail on the ground and the saddest eyes in the world. Sometimes she looks at me as if I've just eaten the last Rolo.

I tell Pepsi everything and she tells me all her secrets. That's how I know she wants puppies! But when I tried to tell Mum that, she said, "Francesca, for the last time, I have told you, the answer is NO! Pepsi is getting too old to have puppies."

"Yeah, even her ears are going grey," said Kenny.

"So?" I said.

"Well, grey ears might stop her winning the Pet Show," said Lyndz.

"Hmm," I said. "I can't see High-Jumping Dog winning either." That's what we sometimes call Lyndz's dog, Buster.

He's got these stumpy little legs, but he can jump up and reach a Smacko even when Lyndz holds it high over her head. It's as if he's got spring-loaded feet. And when he walks he looks like a little clockwork toy.

"I suppose he is a bit wild," Lyndz giggled.

"Jenny's our best hope of winning," said Kenny. "Even though she's a mongrel."

Rosie didn't like Kenny calling Jenny a mongrel. "She's mostly sheepdog," she said. "She can do all sorts of tricks and she's brilliant with Adam."

Adam is Rosie's brother, he's in a wheelchair.

For ages Rosie wouldn't let us go to her house and, like idiots, we thought it was because she felt embarrassed about Adam. Then we found out it was nothing to do with Adam, she was embarrassed because her house was such a tip. Actually, it's not really a tip; it just needs decorating. Now she lets us go round all the time.

Adam can't walk and he can't talk because he's got cerebral palsy, I think that's how you spell it. It means his brain was damaged when he was born, but he's such a laugh. He loves jokes and playing tricks on Rosie. For instance, all their doors swing both ways, so that he can push through in his wheelchair. So he goes through in front of her and then lets it go with his feet so it whips back fast and nearly knocks her over.

Jenny, their dog, seems to know exactly what Adam wants even though he can't talk. She brings him things. And she plays football with him.

Adam's mad about football. He can't use his hands because... I don't know why, they sort of jerk about and he can't stop them. But he can kick a football and Jenny runs after it and brings it back. She's so clever.

Some days, after school, Rosie brings Jenny to the park, where I walk Pepsi. They love playing together and it seems really mean to me just having one dog. I'm an only child so I know how that feels! I've tried telling my mum and dad, but they seem to go deaf whenever I get onto that subject.

But at least I've got a dog. Fliss had no pet to take, as she kept on reminding us.

"It's just not fair, I'm sick of hearing about pet shows."

The Pet Show

Sometimes Fliss is a real moaner. I call her the Mona Lisa.

"At least we've all got one thing to look forward to," I reminded her. "Tomorrow's our first sleepover at Rosie's."

"Humph," Fliss grunted. "It's the night before the Pet Show, so I know what'll happen: you'll be talking about it all night and leaving me out."

"No, we won't," Rosie promised.

"If you like, we won't even mention the word pets," I said.

"Do you promise?" she said, satisfied at last.

The others nodded and made the Brownie promise, but in fact we needn't have bothered, because the next day Rosie had her brainwave about Gazza, the class hamster. And in the end he came to the sleepover too.

CHAPTER THREE

It was Friday, the day before the Pet Show and the day of the sleepover at Rosie's. Kenny and Lyndz had spent the dinner hour cleaning out Gazza's cage. It was their turn on the rota. If you're thinking that Gazza's a dumb name for a hamster, well, it is. The boys in our class chose it. We wanted Cuddles, but we were outvoted.

Fliss had started up *again* about how unfair everything was. So Rosie said, "Fliss, if your mum won't let you have a pet of your own, why don't you ask her if you can take Gazza home one weekend?"

Fliss looked doubtful but everyone else thought it was a great idea.

"Yeah. Neat," said Kenny. "What about this weekend?"

I jumped down to check the rota to see whose turn it was, in case it was someone who might swap with Fliss. "Uh, oh," I said, shaking my head. "It's Alana Banana."

Mrs Weaver walked in just then and gave me one of her looks. She doesn't like us calling each other names, but that is what we call her: Alana Banana Palmer.

"I was just saying, it's Alana's turn to take Gazza home this weekend," I said.

Alana looked up surprised to hear her name, then she went bright pink. She said she'd forgotten to tell Mrs Weaver she couldn't take him, because they were going away for the weekend. I think Alana's really dippy. Mrs Weaver tutted, you could tell she thought so too.

"OK, now we have a problem."

But before anyone else had time to volunteer Emma Hughes pushed to the front.

"That's alright, Mrs Weaver, I'll take him," she said.

"Are you sure, Emma?"

She nodded and gave her one of those *stoopid* sickly smiles she does which make us really mad.

"Oh, yes. It isn't a problem. Mummy won't mind."

But then, suddenly, without asking Fliss about it, Kenny said, "Fliss would like to take him, Mrs Weaver. She's never had a chance before. Emma's taken him lots of times." Emma Hughes gave Kenny such a look but Kenny ignored her.

"Is that true, Felicity?" Mrs Weaver asked. Fliss went pink, but she nodded.

"Do you need to check with your mum?"

Fliss looked doubtful for a moment but Kenny gave her a dig in the ribs. "Oww! No, I think it'll be OK."

"Good. Well, I'm sure Emma doesn't mind if Felicity has a turn," said the teacher, turning round to find the register. "That seems only fair."

The look on the M&Ms' faces was too good to miss. We stood in a row and smiled back at them as if butter wouldn't melt in our mouths, as my gran says.

"Everyone sit down now," said the teacher. We went back to our table feeling really pleased with ourselves.

"Yeah. One-nil!" said Kenny. "That showed those M&Ms."

But Fliss was already looking worried. "I don't know why you made me say that," she hissed at Kenny. "I'll be in real doom when my mum finds out."

That was when Rosie made her great offer: "Don't worry. You can bring him to my house, if you like. You can play with him there and you won't feel so left out."

"Honest?" said Fliss, she couldn't believe her ears. "Won't your mum mind?"

"No," said Rosie. "It'll be fine."

Fliss started to grin. "You're my best friend ever!" she told Rosie.

"Oh, p-lease," I said. Kenny rolled her eyes, Rosie went bright red.

Then Fliss hugged her, which made her even redder. Rosie's still a bit shy of us. She's quite new to our club. She only moved into Cuddington last summer and into our class when we came back after the summer holidays. At first she seemed a bit of a sad case, but then we found out why.

Rosie's dad had left them a few weeks after they moved in, because he'd met someone else. As if that wasn't bad enough, he'd started to do the house up but then just left them in the middle of it. It looked a bit like a building site, really.

That's why Rosie wouldn't let us

sleepover at hers, because everywhere was in a mess, especially her bedroom. We kept telling her it didn't matter and in the end she changed her mind. She gave us these neat invitations. Adam did them for her on his computer. I've still got mine. Do you want to see it?

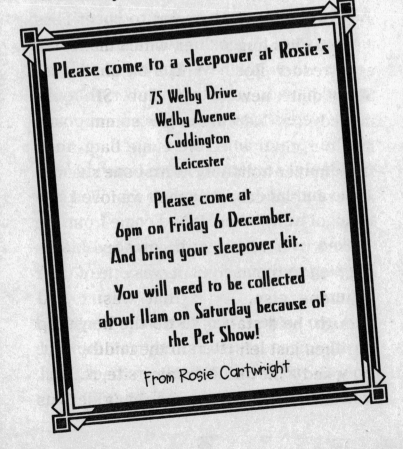

Please come to a sleepover at Rosie's

75 Welby Drive
Welby Avenue
Cuddington
Leicester

Please come at
6pm on Friday 6 December.
And bring your sleepover kit.

You will need to be collected
about 11am on Saturday because of
the Pet Show!

From Rosie Cartwright

I was really looking forward to it because Rosie's house is ever so big with lots of rooms. Some of them are only used for storing stuff, which means loads of places to hide and make dens. It's magic. In fact I couldn't decide which I was more excited about: the Pet Show or the sleepover. Now we'd got the hamster to cheer Fliss up, we were all looking forward to it.

But we might have known the M&Ms would have to go and spoil everything.

We were sitting in our places, supposed to be practising for a spelling test. Suddenly something dive-bombed our table and landed in Kenny's lap. We knew straight away where it had come from. We looked over and saw the dreaded M&Ms giggling to themselves. It was one of their letters.

When we're at war with them they send us the meanest letters they can think of. So we send them nasty letters back. Well, you would, wouldn't you? They print them on the computer so we can't recognise their writing, which is a bit pointless because we know very well it's them and they know very well it's us writing back.

Kenny started to unfold it.

"What does it say?" Fliss squeaked.

"Give me a chance." She smoothed it out and read it aloud to us. "To our enemies. We are watching you. Don't think you'll get away with this. We have put a spell on you. Goodbye forever, Horrible Stinkers."

"What a cheek!" said Lyndz. "We don't stink."

"Right," I said, "after the spelling test we'll ask to go on the computer."

While Mrs Weaver was busy hearing readers, we wrote back to them:

Dear Ugly Mugs,

We hope you both slip down a drain or fall in a bowl of sick. There's no way you will win tomorrow. We'll make sure of that. Have a horrible day, Poshfaces.

31

It's funny really, because that is what happened. Not the bit about them falling down the drain or in a bowl of sick, but about them not winning. When we wrote it we didn't have a plan or anything. It was just one of those things you say. And then, when we met them on the way home from school, we said it again. Afterwards we wished we hadn't, because it all turned out to be true.

CHAPTER FOUR

But hang on, before I tell you about that, let's look for Pepsi in the park, there's a few bushes she likes digging around. I can't see her anywhere yet, can you?

Oh, blow. Not a sign. Now where can we try?

I know: the other place she likes is the canal. I'm not allowed to go there on my own, but Dad and I often walk her there. We could go as far as the bridge next to the pub, you can see a long way down on to the towpath from there.

Come on and I'll tell you what happened next.

By the time we'd collected up all Gazza's bits and pieces, we were a bit late leaving school. Rosie put Gazza into his carrying cage and then we helped her carry everything round to her house. We were already loaded down with PE kit, lunchboxes, and school bags. So we must have looked like a travelling circus when we came round the corner of Mostyn Avenue, which is a couple of roads away from Welby Drive, where Rosie lives. Walking towards us were the gruesome M&Ms and who do you think was with them? Only Ryan Scott and Danny McCloud, two horrible boys from our class. That was all we needed.

"Oh, look, it's the Famous Five," said Emma Hughes.

"Which one's the dog?" said Ryan Scott. He thinks he's so funny.

"Ruff, ruff. Here, girls," shouted Danny

McCloud, "fetch a stick." And he broke a whole branch off a tree by the side of the road and threw it at us. Good job for him he missed.

"Oh, very clever," I said. But they'd both started now, whistling and calling us good dogs and silly things like that. Fliss looked like a boiled beetroot with embarrassment. Fliss actually likes Ryan Scott; she says she wants to marry him! She is so weird.

We just kept on walking, pretending we couldn't hear them, but they followed us.

"Dogs are supposed to be kept on a lead," shouted Ryan Scott.

"I've got a good idea," said Emma Hughes, "they could enter each other for the Pet Show. That way they might win."

"Well, you're not gonna win, that's for sure," said Kenny.

"That's what you think," said The Goblin.

"That's what we *know*," said Rosie.

"And how are you going to stop us?" said The Queen.

"Don't you worry, we have our ways," I said, mysteriously.

We all smiled at each other, as if we'd got this big secret that they knew nothing about. We walked off down the road.

"What ways?" Emma Hughes shouted after us.

"You'll find out," Kenny called back to her. Then we carried on down the road trying to ignore the fact that those two stupid dodos were still whistling us to come and the gruesome M&Ms were giggling at them as if they were the funniest things on legs.

Fliss turned to Kenny, "How *are* we going to stop them?"

Kenny shrugged. "Don't ask me," she said, "ask Frankie."

I shrugged too. I had no idea either. But, we'd got them worried and that was almost as good.

The Pet Show

* * *

When we reached Rosie's, she was right, her mum didn't mind about Gazza.

"What difference can a hamster make?" she said. "It'll be enough of a madhouse with all you girls round." But she smiled, so we knew she was only kidding.

We were all so excited to be sleeping over at a different house, we raced off home to get our things packed. "See you at seven," Rosie called after us. "Don't be late."

When I got home I gave Pepsi an extra good brush and clean up and told Mum and Dad they'd better keep her like that.

"Don't let her roll in anything on her walk tonight," I warned them.

"Yes, boss," said Dad. "Any more orders while you're away?"

"Yes," I said. "Kindly collect me at eleven in the morning. And don't be late!"

When we arrived at Rosie's we went

straight upstairs and dumped our sleepover kits on her bedroom floor. She's right, her room does look a bit funny with no wallpaper, just plaster on the walls, but her mum lets her put posters up, so it doesn't look boring; it's dead colourful in fact. She's got Oasis, Blur and loads of pictures of dogs and people out of the soaps on her walls. Rosie's soppy about soaps.

Her dad's promised to come round soon and decorate, so her mum says she's allowed to write on the walls, which none of the rest of us are allowed to do in our bedrooms.

Rosie said we could help her if we wanted to. It was so cool. We wrote loads of jokes, like *What did the spaceman see in his frying pan? An unidentified frying object. And What do you do if you find a blue banana? Try to cheer it up.*

Rosie said it would certainly cheer her up, when she was lying in bed at night, to read those jokes.

"Just think," I said, "in about a zillion years…"

"When the aliens come," said Lyndz.

"…they might take the wallpaper off and find these jokes."

So then we got into writing messages to Martians and it all got a bit silly. One of them was a bit rude. We had to scribble it out before Rosie's mum saw it. It's a good job we did because just then she came in to tell us to come down for tea.

"Great," said Kenny, "I'm ravishing."

"Don't you mean ravenous?" said Rosie's mum

"I'm ravishing, too," said Kenny, pulling one of her silly faces.

"You're weird, you mean," I said. Then she chased me downstairs to the kitchen. Rosie's mum had laid out a great spread for us with paper cups and plates and fancy serviettes, just like a party. She's dead nice. She's going to college to learn to be a nursery nurse. Rosie has an older sister, Tiffany, but she's always out with her boyfriend, Spud. Her brother Adam was there, though. We're really getting used to Adam now. It was strange at first, talking to someone who can't talk back to you, but Rosie's mum can tell us what he wants to say because he sort of spells it out with his head and she can understand him. So can Rosie some of the time, if he does it slowly.

We had pizza and salad and oven chips, and ice cream for afters. The pizza was OK, but it wasn't a patch on my dad's. The ice cream was heavenly, though: pecan and toffee fudge. Mmm, mmm. Rosie's mum sat and fed Adam, because he can't feed himself, and then she sat him on her knee to give him a drink through one of those baby feeder cups. All the time we were eating he was watching us and listening to what we were saying.

"What are you grinning at?" Rosie said.

Adam stopped drinking because he was choking a bit.

"That's what comes of trying to drink and grin at the same time," said his mum. Then Adam started shaking his head. He was trying to spell something. It was a poem he'd made up, while he'd been watching us have tea. Rosie says he's always making up poems... and jokes. Rosie's mum started spelling it out.

"F-I-V... Five?" she said. Adam nodded then spelt out some more.

"Little... Piggies? Sitting... in... a... row? R-O-S... Rosie's the F-A-T-T..." Rosie started to squeal, "Tell him to stop."

Her mum grinned. "OK, young man, that's enough. Remember your manners."

"You're the little piggy," Rosie told Adam.

"That's about right," their mum said, wiping his chin.

After we'd eaten Rosie said we could

explore her house. There are five bedrooms on the first floor, then a staircase which leads to two more rooms, right up in the roof. In places, I could only just stand up straight without banging my head on the ceiling. The rooms were full of packing cases, cardboard boxes and old bits of furniture. There were no light bulbs up there, so when it started to get dark we couldn't turn on the lights and that made it really spooky.

We played Hide and Seek and Murder in the Dark all over the upstairs and in the attic rooms, squealing and rushing around. There were no light–bulbs up there so we had to use our torches and that made it really spooky. But in no time it was nine o'clock and Rosie's mum came to tell us to get ready for bed. We didn't argue. Actually, we were looking forward to going to bed. That's the best bit.

CHAPTER FIVE

Rosie's room only has one bed in it but it's a double bed. It's coo-ell. None of the rest of us has a doule bed. She's so lucky. We all tried to fit into it, like playing Sardines; we just piled on top of each other. But there was no way we could sleep like that.

"Give me some room," yelled Kenny who was right in the middle. "It's too hot in here."

"I'm falling out," yelled Lyndz.

"Can't you breathe in?" yelled Rosie.

"All night?" I said. "Get real."

So in the end we decided two of us would have to sleep in sleeping bags on the floor. We tossed for it. Oh, g-reat. Guess who lost? Me, of course. And Fliss, who moaned on and on about how it wasn't fair, even though it really was.

After we'd been in the bathroom we sat up in our sleeping bags with our sleepover diaries. At least the rest of us did; Fliss was too busy playing with Gazza.

Kenny was scribbling away like mad, she'd finished before I'd even thought about mine. She slammed her diary shut. "That's me done," she said.

"Read us what you've put," said Lyndz.

"What's it worth?" she said, which is Kenny's favourite question.

"If you do, I'll let you hold Gazza while I write mine," said Fliss.

"Oh, great big hairy deal," said Kenny. But then she said, "OK."

She started to read hers out: "Today is Friday. We are sleeping over at Rosie's house for the first time and it is awesome. I wish I lived here. It's the best." Rosie started to smile; she was dead pleased with that. "Tomorrow, we are going to the Pet Show at the Village Hall and if Merlin wins a rosette I will tie it to his tail. We are at war with the M&Ms... again. They had better look out." She slammed her diary shut and said. "Now, give, give, give, give, give." She held out her hands for the hamster.

"You promised you weren't going to talk about *that*," complained Fliss. But she passed Gazza over while she wrote hers.

Then everyone wanted a turn, so we played Pass the Hamster for a bit. When Rosie went to the bathroom she brought back a toilet roll which was just about used up. She tossed it onto the bed and Kenny put Gazza down so he could wriggle through it, like a tunnel but he seemed more interested in filling his pouches with it.

Next Fliss read us what she'd written: "I haven't got a pet to take to the you-know-what so Rosie is letting me keep Gazza at her house. It is very kind of her. She is my best friend. She can take him out and play with him whenever she likes – as long as she is careful."

Kenny looked at me and rolled her eyes. Sometimes Fliss is unreal. It was then that Rosie came up with her other idea. To tell you the truth, it wasn't such a good idea, but at first we thought it was.

"Why not take Gazza tomorrow?" she said to Fliss. "You can pretend he's yours. No one'll know."

"Yeah, why not?" said Kenny.

I nodded too. I thought it was a great idea, because, if Fliss had a pet to take, it would mean we could talk about the Pet Show, without her moaning on.

"I don't know," said Fliss, doubtfully,

"what if someone recognises him?"

"How would they?" said Rosie. "One hamster looks much like another."

"What if there's anyone from school there?"

We thought about that. It was unlikely our teacher, Mrs Weaver, would be there, but what about other people from our class? And then, as if it had dawned on us all at once, I said, "Oh, no..." and everyone joined in, "The M&Ms."

They'd be sure to recognise Gazza. Those two didn't miss a thing.

"Oh, well, it was a good idea while it lasted," I said.

"Hang on," said Kenny, "You could keep him in a box, or something, until they do the judging. The M&Ms'll be too busy with their own pets. They'll probably be in different rooms. I doubt if they'll put the cats and dogs together with the small pets."

"Yeah. Good thinking, Batman," I said.

You could see Fliss was tempted, but she was still worried about it. Fliss always gets her knickers in a twist if she does anything wrong in case she gets found out. But she really wanted to join in with the rest of us, so in the end she said, "OK, but you've all got to promise not to tell anyone, though."

We all made the Brownie promise and just then Rosie's mum came in and told us to turn off the lights and settle down. I was sure she hadn't heard us but Fliss went bright pink, as if Rosie's mum could read her mind. When she got up to put Gazza in his cage, she dropped him twice. Fortunately both times he landed on the bed. At last she put him in his cage, but she was so nervous she didn't fasten the cage door properly. It was nearly an hour before we realised and by then Gazza had completely disappeared.

After Rosie's mum went out we lay in bed

and counted to twenty-five before we sat up. Sitting up in the dark, with our torches turned on, whispering, is the best thing about sleepovers, I think. Sometimes we tell stories or sing songs or tell jokes. Sometimes we pretend we can talk to ghosts but that can get a bit too scary. Later on, when it's really quiet and we know the grown-ups aren't coming back in, we get out our midnight feast. But it was too early so we decided to finish off our Sleepover Club membership cards.

We'd got some old ones we'd made right at the beginning, but now Rosie's joined we decided we'd make some new ones with photos and everything.

Do you want to see mine? Isn't it excellent? Not as good as Fliss's, though. Hers looks dead posh. She got her mum to take her into Leicester to get a proper passport photo done. The rest of us had to cut up old photographs. I had to cut my face out of a picture at my Uncle Alan's wedding when I was little. Everybody started laughing at it, so I told them what my gran always says, "Small things amuse small minds!"

On the back of the cards we wrote our names, ages, addresses and hobbies. When we'd finished them we signed them. Well, the rest of us did. Kenny did this weird squiggle that looked as if someone had nudged her elbow. Then we passed them round and read each others'.

"I didn't know your hobby was stamp collecting," I said to Fliss.

She went a bit red. "It isn't but I didn't know what else to put. I don't really have a hobby."

"Course you do," said Lyndz. "You go to Brownies, don't you? You go to dancing classes and gymnastics. You're interested in fashion." She reeled off a few more.

"Oh, I didn't realise *they* were hobbies," said Fliss, grabbing her card back. She's so dozy. She scribbled away and soon ran out of space.

For my hobbies I wrote: Reading, Brownies, Pop Music, Collecting Teddies and Acting. I just *lurv* being in plays. It's the best.

Kenny had written: Football, Swimming, Gymnastics, Snooker, Brownies.

Rosie had put: Netball, (I'd forgotten that), Soaps (she's mad about them), Pop Music and Brownies.

Next I read Lyndz's. She'd written: Horses, Painting, Horses, Brownies, Horses, Cooking Horses.

"Cooking horses?" I said.

"Let me see that." She grabbed it back from me. She'd just missed out the comma. "Oh, very funny, I don't think."

I thought it was very funny, actually, and so did Kenny. We creased up.

Later on, when we were sure Rosie's mum wasn't coming back, we got out the food, put it in a big bowl and passed it round. I'll tell you what there was: sherbet dabs, Black Jacks, Love Hearts, a Snickers bar, six marshmallows and a packet of Original Pringles. We all tucked in straight away.

"D'you think we should give Gazza something?" said Fliss.

"It doesn't seem fair leaving him out," Rosie agreed.

But really there was nothing apart from Pringles we thought a hamster might eat and we weren't really sure about those. We decided we'd try him just with a couple of crumbs to see. Fliss got out of her sleeping bag and went to get him.

That's when we realised he'd gone.

CHAPTER SIX

"He's not here," she wailed. "Oh, help, where is he?"

I jumped up as well, just to check, because Fliss is always losing things, even when they're staring her in the face, but this time she was right: he wasn't there. And when we turned on the lights he wasn't anywhere else we could see either.

We stripped everything off the bed and searched all five sleeping bags. We looked under the bed. We emptied all our sleepover kits out in a pile in the middle of the floor. There were leggings and T-shirts and socks and knickers and slippers and toilet bags and torches and hairbrushes and teddies and sweet packets from the midnight feast. And we still couldn't find him.

Fliss was nearly wetting herself. She kept saying over and over, "I'm going to be in such trouble with Mrs Weaver. I'm going to be in doom forever."

And just then Rosie's mum came back in. "My goodness, what's all this noise?" she said. "Whatever's going on?"

So then we had to tell her, Gazza was gone.

She helped us search the room all over again. But in the end she said, "Well, there's nothing else we can do tonight. We'll just have to hope he comes back when he's hungry. The door's been closed, so he must still be in the room somewhere. We'd just better make sure Jenny doesn't get in here tonight."

"Oh, no," said Fliss horrified. "Would she eat him?"

"Probably not, but the poor hamster might die of fright if he saw her."

"But where can he have gone?" said Fliss, nearly in tears.

"We've looked everywhere, Mum," said Rosie.

"He could be under the floorboards, who knows. Come on, now, let's have this light off and you girls settle down."

"I don't want to sleep on the floor any more," said Fliss.

"I'll swap with you," said Rosie.

So Fliss dragged her sleeping bag onto the bed and Rosie and I got into our sleeping bags on the floor. We cuddled our teddies and Rosie's mum turned out the light.

"It's very late," she said, "I think you should try to go to sleep, now. Goodnight."

For quite a long time, we all lay in the

dark and no one spoke. Rosie kept turning over, Lyndz sucked her thumb, Fliss was sniffing a bit. It sounded as if she was crying. Then I heard Lyndz whisper, "Don't worry. He'll turn up."

"But what if he doesn't?" Fliss sniffed. "I'll be left out again."

I felt sorry for Fliss too but I didn't know what to do. I turned over and tried to get to sleep. I'm always the last to drop off. My brain won't seem to go to sleep for ages after I go to bed, so I was lying there, thinking everyone else was asleep by now, when I heard this noise. It was quite close. In fact it sounded as if it was right underneath my pillow, right under my ear.

Rosie whispered, "Frankie, are you awake?"

"Yes," I whispered.

"Can you hear that noise?"

I could and I knew exactly what it was: Gazza was on the move.

I sat up and turned on my torch. We

crawled out of our sleeping bags and pulled back the carpet. Rosie doesn't have a fitted carpet, like the one in my bedroom. She just has this big square rug in the middle of the floor. We rolled up one side of it and followed the sound and shone our torches down the crack between the floorboards.

"I think I can see him," Rosie hissed. We both got so excited we banged heads. "OW," I yelled. Suddenly all the others were awake.

"What's going on?" said Kenny, jumping out of bed.

"Is it morning?" said Lyndz, rubbing her eyes. She'd only been asleep ten minutes!

"I'm sure I can see him," Rosie said again.

I wasn't sure I could, but I could certainly hear him moving about. Soon the others were crowding round us, Fliss was shivering in her nightie.

"Move back," I said. "You're in the light."

"Try and coax him out with some Pringles," said Kenny, getting one and crumbling it between her fingers. "Look what we've got for you," she said, poking the crumbs down between the floorboards. She posted as much through as she could and waited. But still nothing happened. So we tried some more, until we'd pushed a whole Pringle down.

"If you keep pushing food through to him he'll never come out," said Rosie. "In fact if he eats too much he might get so fat he can't fit back through the hole."

"Good thinking, Wonder Woman," I said. Rosie's pretty clever at times.

Next we tried tapping messages on the floorboards above his head and flashing our torches on and off. But we couldn't get him to come out.

Then Kenny got silly and started shining her torch up Fliss's nightdress.

Fliss shouted, "That's not fair, just because I'm the only one in a nightdress."

So then we shone them up each other's pyjama legs instead, until Rosie hissed at us, "Shhh, my mum'll be in and then there'll be trouble."

I was ready to get back into my sleeping bag anyway, I was getting cold.

"Let's finish off our midnight feast," said Lyndz. But first I made a little trail of food.

Rosie's mum had said Gazza would soon come back if he got hungry. So we crushed up the last few Pringles - there were only three left but as Kenny pointed out that would be a feast for a hamster - and laid them in a trail from the spot where we had heard him, all the way back to his cage.

When all the food was gone Lyndz started dozing off again. Lyndz is always the first to go to sleep. She'd already got her thumb in her mouth and her eyes kept closing. Kenny dug her in the ribs. "Wake up," she said, "let's sing our song before you nod off."

We've got this Sleepover song that we always sing before we go to sleep. I bet you've heard it before.

Down by the river there's a hanky panky

With a bullfrog sitting on the hanky panky

With an Ooh, Aah, Ooh, Aah,

Hey, Mrs Zippy, with a One-two-three...Out!

At the end of each verse one of us lies down. This time I was the one left sitting up in the dark on my own. It felt scary, but in a nice way. You know what I mean?

I turned off my torch and snuggled down into my sleeping bag. I must have fallen asleep straight away and I didn't wake up until the morning, even though I had a horrid dream about being chased down tunnels by hamsters with pouches full of Pringles.

CHAPTER SEVEN

The next morning there was still no sign of Gazza. When I first woke up, I thought he'd come back. Fliss was squealing as if he was crawling over her face or something. In fact it was Kenny up to her tricks. She was using Fliss's pony tail to tickle her neck. The first couple of times Fliss just brushed it away, without opening her eyes. Then she must have woken up and remembered the hamster on the loose because she just started to squeal, "AGGHHHH!" After that we were all awake and on the move.

One of the other great things about Rosie's house is the wide staircase. We had mega sleeping-bag races sliding down on our bottoms two at a time. It was excellent until we had to stop because Lyndz split her sleeping bag. She wasn't worried because it was an absolutely ancient one that used to be her brother's. It was already in holes and she was dying for a new one. I'd have been in BIG trouble.

Then we made up a new game for our International Gladiators Challenge. We took it in turns to do a mad dash down the stairs, past the others armed with pillows or squishy poos. (A squishy poo is a sleeping bag filled with clothes for whacking people with.) It was magic!

Adam sat in his chair in the kitchen doorway watching us and bouncing up and down with excitement. We all felt sorry that he couldn't join in and afterwards Lyndz said we should make up some special events that he *could* join in with, which I thought was a neat idea. At least Adam was coming with us to the Pet Show later because, after all, Jenny's really his dog.

We were having such a great time none of us wanted to go home when our parents came to collect us. But we had to because we all needed to get our pets organised.

Gazza still hadn't turned up by the time we left, but Rosie's mum said, "Don't worry we'll keep on searching."

Fliss looked dead miserable. She said there was no point in her going home because she didn't have a pet to get ready. As if we didn't all know that!

Rosie said "You could stay here and help us look for him, if you want to." So that cheered her up a bit.

* * *

When I got home Mum was giving Pepsi a bath, which she hates. She doesn't like water at all. She never jumps in the river like other dogs, she even runs away if Dad turns the hose pipe on in the garden. So I had to hold on to her to keep her in the bath, while Mum shampooed her and then rinsed her off. Then, even though we put the gas fire on and sat her in front of it, she shivered as if she was freezing. Dad rubbed her until she was nearly dry and then I brushed her.

We had to trim some tangled bits of fur from her ears. They do get messy because they hang down in everything. But Dad said, "Never worry. You won't see from a distance."

When we'd finished, she looked so adorable, I told her it didn't matter what the judges thought. I thought she was the most beautiful dog in the world. And I gave her a big hug and she gave me a big lick.

The Pet Show

* * *

We'd arranged to meet at the Village Hall at two o'clock. Brown Owl told us the hall wouldn't open until two-thirty but we couldn't wait to get there. I was first because Mum and Dad dropped me off on their way to the supermarket. They said they'd come back later to watch us. It was starting to rain, but I'd got my kagoul on.

I took Pepsi onto the field behind the Village Hall for a few minutes and then she sat down patiently near the entrance, while we waited for the others. My tummy was full of butterflies. I was already feeling excited and now I was starting to feel a bit nervous so I was glad when Kenny's dad drove up and dropped her off.

Kenny was in her Brownie uniform, the same as me, and she was carrying Merlin in a brown cardboard box with holes in the lid. Her dad had made a rope handle so she could carry it without Merlin turning somersaults inside. She lifted the lid to show me, but I just took a quick peep and kept my distance. Pepsi was much more interested than I was but we tried to keep her away because whenever she got close to the box we could hear Merlin racing round in circles, scrabbling to get out.

Rosie came next with Fliss. They were walking towards us and Fliss wasn't carrying anything, so Kenny said to me, "Uh-oh, it doesn't look as if Gazza's turned up." But even from a distance we could see she was smiling.

"Have you got him?" I shouted to her.

She frowned at me, as if I'd said something wrong. When she got closer she hissed, "Do you want to tell everyone? It's supposed to be a secret, remember."

Kenny said, "There's nobody here, yet."

"No, but walls have ears," she said. Then she stood close up to us and held her kagoul pocket open. We peeped in and there he was, a bit dusty-looking, but otherwise OK.

"How did you get him out?" whispered Kenny.

"We had to take the floorboard up in the end. It was Adam's idea."

"Where is Adam?"

"Mum's bringing him later. Where's Lyndz?"

But we just shrugged, there was no sign of her yet.

You could tell Jenny and Pepsi were pleased to see each other, their tails were wagging nineteen to the dozen. We would have liked to take them onto the field and let them off their leads but we wanted to keep them nice and clean, so we tried to get them to sit and be good. And they were, until Buster came. Then the trouble started.

Buster isn't used to being on a lead; he was pulling so hard Lyndz couldn't control him. He's only a quarter of the size of Pepsi and Jenny but he's so strong. The minute he saw them he made a bee-line for them. He wouldn't stop fussing and jumping up at them.

"Leave them alone, Buster," Lyndz kept saying. But he wouldn't. He was a menace. Then he noticed Kenny's box and started growling at it. We could hear Merlin scuffling about inside, as if he knew there was an enemy outside, which there was. The minute Lyndz pulled Buster away from Kenny, he started fussing Fliss and getting up on his back legs to reach her pocket.

"Get him off," Fliss squealed.

"I'm trying," said Lyndz, yanking on Buster's lead.

Thank goodness it wasn't long before Brown Owl arrived.

"You girls are very early," she said. "Well, you'd better come inside, out of the rain, but you'll have to wait in the foyer until we're set up. Please keep your pets under control."

"That's what I'm trying to do," said Lyndz, under her breath. But she wasn't having much success.

A few other people were beginning to arrive, so we followed them into the building. But when we got into the foyer and saw who was sitting there, behind a table, ready to take everyone's names, we nearly went home again. It was Snowy Owl, and, in case you've forgotten who Snowy Owl is, she's only Fliss's Auntie Jill. She knew Fliss didn't have her own hamster. Why hadn't we thought about her?

Fliss turned straight round and raced outside, and the rest of us followed her.

CHAPTER EIGHT

"What am I going to do now?" Fliss wailed.

"Look, what are you worried about?" I said. "You haven't done anything wrong."

"Not yet," said Fliss.

"Why not just keep him in your pocket?" said Lyndz. "No one need know."

"Oh, that's all right for you to say, but I was really looking forward to this. I want to be in the Pet Show."

Poor old Fliss, we all wanted her to be in the Pet Show too, but we couldn't think of a way to help. It was raining harder now and we were getting properly wet. But I remembered what my gran always says, where there's a will, there must be a way. I concentrated really hard.

Rosie was standing by Fliss, patting her shoulder. "This is all my fault," she said. "I shouldn't have had that stupid idea in the first place."

"It was a good idea," said Lyndz. "You weren't to know."

"I've got it," I said. "We'll tell Snowy Owl he's Rosie's hamster. She can't take him in because she's got Jenny as well. So you're going to enter him for her."

"Yeah! One-nil!" said Kenny. "Mega-Brain Strikes Again."

"Oh, Frankie, you're so clever," said Rosie.

Mmm, yes, I thought, I am pretty cool, actually.

"OK, let's go," I said. It was nearly two thirty and lots more people were arriving.

But when we went back into the foyer,

we nearly had to come out again, because now there wasn't just Snowy Owl at the desk, her boyfriend, Dishy Dave was there too. Dishy Dave's the caretaker at school. He might recognise Gazza, because he's always in and out of our classroom, checking up on things.

Fliss was about to disappear again, so I grabbed her.

"Just keep him in your pocket," I whispered.

"And try to look natural," whispered Kenny.

Fliss swallowed and gave a big sigh. "I wished I'd stayed at home," she said. But she didn't really, you could tell.

When we got to the front of the queue I went first and gave my name.

"And your dog's?" said Snowy Owl, busy writing.

"Pepsi," I said, smiling.

"What class?" she asked me.

"Class?" I didn't know what she meant.

"Obedience? Appearance? Novelty?"

Well, I knew Pepsi wasn't very obedient so I chose Appearance. Snowy Owl gave me a card with a large number nine on it. "Dogs are in the Main Hall," she said. "Listen for your name to be called."

Rosie chose Obedience as well as Appearance because Jenny's very well-behaved and comes whenever you call her. She got a number ten to hold.

When it came to Lyndz she didn't know which to choose for Buster. He's quite a funny looking thing, not a bit pretty and he certainly doesn't do as he's told.

Snowy Owl told her she'd put him in Obedience because there weren't many dogs in that class, and Novelty too. Buster was number eleven, which made me giggle.

"What's so funny?" said Lyndz.

"You know," I said. "In Bingo, when they call out 'Legs Eleven'. It really suits him." But Lyndz wasn't amused.

Then it was Kenny's turn. "Laura

McKenzie and Merlin," said Kenny.

"And what's Merlin?" asked Snowy Owl, looking at the box.

"My white rat," said Kenny, opening the lid to show her. Snowy Owl went white and leant back in her chair. You could see she wasn't keen on rats. She looked as if she was having trouble swallowing.

"That's alright. I don't need to see him. Just keep him in the box until the judges are ready. Number twelve, room three: small animals."

"Are there any other rats entered?" I asked.

"Not at the moment," said Snowy. "Thank goodness," she added, under her breath.

"So if nobody else comes," said Dave, "you'll win automatically."

That made Kenny grin. Jammy or what!

Then it was Fliss's turn. She was looking very pink. Snowy Owl smiled at her. "I think I know your name," she said.

Well, she ought to, she's her auntie, after all. "Are you just here to keep your friends company?"

Fliss didn't know what to say.

"No," I said for her, "she's entering Rosie's hamster."

Snowy Owl looked at Dave. "Well, I suppose that's allowed."

"Yeah," said Dave. "Why not?" And he winked at us. "We won't tell anyone."

"So, where is he?"

"In her pocket," said Rosie. Snowy Owl frowned.

"Oh, it's OK, he likes it," said Kenny.

"Well, what's his name?"

Fliss looked at Rosie, who looked straight at me. Why do people always expect me to come up with ideas? My mind went to jelly for a second or two, then I suddenly said, "Hammy."

"Hammy the Hamster?" said Dave, not very impressed. But Snowy Owl wrote it down. "Room three, with Kenny. Here's your number."

Fliss looked at the number she was holding out and almost burst into tears. "Sorry about that," said her Auntie Jill. "Luck of the draw, I'm afraid."

We moved away from the table, into the corridor.

"Number Thirteen. Just my luck," said Fliss.

"Well, at least we've got the first bit over," I said. It might have been the first, but it wasn't the worst. That came later.

The door opened. Suddenly we could hear everyone oohing and aahing and making a fuss in the foyer. Who do you think had just walked in? Yes, you've guessed: the dreaded M&Ms. And when we saw Emma Hughes's dog, we nearly all went home.

I'd never seen a dog so white. You almost needed sunglasses to look at her. Rosie, who knows about different kinds of dogs, said she was a husky. Her fur was long and soft and she looked as if she'd had a bath in milk. So this was the famous Duchess of Drumshaw The Third.

You could see straight away she was going to win. Everyone was saying, "Oh, what a beautiful dog! Oh, isn't she absolutely gorgeous." And other sickly things like that. I'm not saying she wasn't a really cute dog, but so are Pepsi and Jenny and no one was making a fuss of them.

Emma Hughes just stood there wearing that *stoopid* face of hers, smiling, as if they were talking about her! When she gave her name in she said, "Which name would you like, her pedigree name or her ordinary, everyday name?"

"What do you usually call her?" Snowy Owl asked.

Then Emma Hughes and Emily Berryman started to giggle. We didn't know what was so funny, until she said. "We call her Snowball." And then she giggled again. Oh, yuk!

"Oh," said Snowy Owl. "That's a good name."

After that she made a big fuss of Emily Berryman's cat. Snowy Owl's a real cat-lover. It was a Siamese, called Smoky. It was so thin it didn't look very well to me. It had this blue ribbon round its neck with a little bell on it and Snowy Owl thought it was lovely.

"OK. Number twenty-one, Emily," she said. "Room two for cats. Go straight along. They'll be starting soon."

We all went off to the rooms we'd been sent to. When those of us with dogs got down to the hall, Brown Owl let us go in, a few at a time. She showed us what we'd have to do, then we had a little practice, before the judges arrived.

It was nearly time for the whole thing to start. I kept looking out for Mum and Dad. I didn't want them to be late and miss seeing me walk Pepsi round in front of the judges. But they came in just before three o'clock. They arrived at the same time as Rosie's mum and Adam.

Adam was dead excited; he kept jiggling in his chair, which got Jenny a bit excited too. Once or twice I noticed Emily Hughes staring at Adam, and I think Rosie did, but she ignored her. I think that's the best thing to do with people like her.

CHAPTER NINE

Just after three o'clock the first people went in with their dogs for the Obedience class. All the parents went in and sat on chairs round the outside of the hall to watch but Brown Owl said I couldn't go in with Pepsi because she might distract the other dogs. I knew she wouldn't, but there was no point arguing with Brown Owl. She was looking a bit stressed out. Instead, I went down the corridor and peeped into the small pets room. They wouldn't let me go in there, either. I suppose they thought

Pepsi might try to eat the small pets or something, so I just hung around the door.

There were lots of little children with hamsters and gerbils and guinea pigs and rabbits, but so far Kenny was the only person who'd brought a rat. She came over to the door to talk to me and she was looking pretty pleased with herself. But then this big boy from the High School wearing a leather jacket pushed past us with a cage with two humungous black rats inside. They made Merlin look like a mouse. Kenny was fed up, but I told her what my gran always says, "It's quality that counts, not quantity."

"Hmmm," she said, not cheered up at all. "I just hope the judges know that."

Fliss was enjoying herself. She was sitting on a chair in the corner with two or three little girls from the Infants, letting them stroke Gazza.

The judges were looking at the rabbits

first; they hadn't started on hamsters yet.

One of the organisers spotted me at the door. She came over, waving her hand for me to go away. "Dogs are in the Main Hall," she said, as if I didn't know, so I went back to the foyer to wait until it was my turn.

There were lots of people waiting outside the hall, including Emma Hughes. Pepsi would have liked to go and get to know her dog, Snowball, but I pulled her away. And then The Goblin came along holding her cat. I was so mad when I saw she was wearing a red rosette on her collar. On it was a big 1st.

Emma Hughes started squealing and then the two of them stood whispering and giggling together, looking over at me, but I pretended not to notice. Suddenly the hall door opened and out came Buster dragging Lyndz behind him. Lyndz looked really pink and she had the hiccups!

"How did you get on?" I asked.

"D-d-don't ask," Lyndz hiccupped. "He nearly bit the judges."

Just then, Kenny came along, waving a green rosette.

"We won," she squealed. "We came third."

I said, "Fantastic!" And it was. She'd got a rosette, which was what she wanted, but that stuck-up Emma Hughes said, "Third out of three's nothing to brag about."

How did she know there were only three rats? That's another thing about the M&Ms, they seem to know everything that happens. But Rosie and Adam came out next with Jenny who'd won a blue rosette, because she'd come second for good behaviour. So that showed those two!

Lyndz was still hiccupping and Buster was starting to jump up at Kenny's box again.

"Oh— hic— stop it," Lyndz snapped at

him. But he didn't.

"He's a very obedient dog, isn't he?" said Emily Berryman, sarcastically.

Then Buster stopped jumping up and down and turned round and started pulling towards her, just as if he'd heard what she'd said, and wanted to give her a piece of his mind. But I think it was because he'd just caught sight of her cat. And then the trouble really started.

Buster's hackles went up and he was barking so loudly that all four feet lifted off the ground at once. And then, without any warning, he leapt forward, pulling so hard he snapped his lead, which was a pretty old one anyway, and catapulted himself forward to get at the cat. But he missed and landed on Snowball's back. He looked like a little circus dog landing on a horse. It frightened Snowball so much that she leapt sideways, tipping Buster off, and then she panicked and charged out of the foyer, towards the front doors, pulling Emma behind her. Buster was snapping at her heels.

There were lots of people standing near to the door and a lady with a little boy in a buggy was trying to get in, but Snowball was too panicked to wait, so the lady had to. They all collided, Emma tripped over the buggy, the lead slipped through her fingers and in a second Snowball was gone.

Everyone ran after them shouting, "Stop that dog!" and things like that. The next minute we were all outside the building, in the rain, chasing Emma and Lyndz who were trying to catch their dogs. Emily was running, holding onto her cat; I was running with Pepsi; Rosie was running with Jenny; Kenny was running carrying Merlin in his box; even Fliss had joined us by now with Gazza in her pocket.

We were worried at first that the dogs might run out onto the road, but luckily they headed round the side of the building instead and onto the field behind. The faster Snowball ran away, the more determined Buster was to catch her. I don't think he was really interested in Snowball, it was the chase he was enjoying. He was so excited, he'd have chased anything on legs that was running.

They ran right to the bottom of the field, through every puddle on the way. And then they dodged through a hole in the hedge into the sports field and disappeared for a while, although we could hear them both barking their heads off.

Emma and Lyndz were shouting their heads off, too, and so were the rest of us, which Brown Owl told us later was the biggest mistake we made. She said that would have just made them even more excited. And it did. They were wild.

We stopped running when we lost sight of them, but a minute later they popped back through the hedge in a different place and we all started running again.

I don't think we'd ever have caught up with them, if they hadn't turned full circle and headed back towards the Village Hall. But we still weren't quick enough to stop them heading towards the huge pile of coke that was stacked behind the Hall.

"Oh, no! Snowball! Come back!" Emma yelled. But Snowball didn't. She just charged up to it and then raced to the top of it and Buster followed her. The pile of coke collapsed under them and they sank into it, up to their shoulders.

"Snowball! No! No!" It wasn't so much a shout this time, as a wail. By the time Emma reached her, Snowball's coat was covered with coke. And so was Buster's.

Lyndz jumped into the middle and sank down to her knees, but she managed to grab Buster's collar and yank him out with one hand, and grab Snowball with the other one. She pulled them both out.

But when Emma saw the state of her dog, instead of saying thank you to Lyndz, she started screaming at her and telling her it was all her fault. Lyndz tried to say she was sorry, lots of times, but she couldn't finish her sentence.

"It was just an... He didn't really mean... He's quite a nice... dog really."

But Emma Hughes kept interrupting her. Emily Berryman was patting her on the shoulder and trying to calm her down but it wasn't working.

"You did this on purpose," Emma screamed at Lyndz. "You planned this to stop me from winning. You were all in on it."

"No," Lyndz said again. "It was an accident. Honest."

"I don't believe you," she yelled at her. She turned to Emily. "You heard them. They said they'd got something planned, didn't they? They're going to be in real trouble. All of them."

Emily nodded. "Come on," she said. "Let's go and tell Brown Owl."

But instead of going with her, Emma burst out crying. It was awful. We didn't know what to do. We didn't know what to say, either. We just stood there watching her cry in the rain.

The truth is we hadn't had a plan. It was an accident. Lyndz hadn't set Buster onto Snowball, it had been entirely his own idea. Lyndz would have stopped him, if she could. And she did feel bad about it. We all did. The poor dog looked an awful mess. Her feet and legs were splashed with mud and her coat was thick with coke dust. Rosie tried to brush a bit of it off with her hand, but now Snowball's coat was wet, it just smeared everywhere and looked even worse. Jenny and Pepsi sniffed round her sympathetically.

"Get off!" Emma screamed. "Keep away from her." She was nearly in hysterics. "Take those horrible... mutts away."

Mutts! Rosie and I looked at each other and burst out laughing. We tried not to but it just came out. Then Lyndz started and her hiccups came back.

"I think you're all horrible," Emily Berryman said to us and she pulled Emma away and they went back into the Village Hall to find Brown Owl.

"Uh, oh," said Kenny, trying to keep a straight face. "That's put the king in the cake."

"You mean that's put The Queen in the cake," I said. And that set us all off again.

ALL'S WELL THAT ENDS WELL

When we got back in everyone was shouting for us. It seems they'd called out our names for the Appearance class two or three times already. We had to go straight in, even though we were soaking wet and so were the dogs. They didn't look their best, especially Snowball. But it was good fun and in fact, by the end of the afternoon, we'd all won at least one rosette.

Kenny had won her green rosette for coming third with Merlin. Fliss won a special prize for "Hammy" for being the Tamest Hamster in the Show. He was very well behaved and let everyone stroke him. Jenny had already won a blue rosette for coming second in the Most Obedient Dog class and then she won another rosette for being the Dog the Judges Would Most Like to Take Home With Them. Pepsi won a rosette for the Dog With the Most Appealing Eyes. I told you she was cute, didn't I?

And you'll never believe this, but Buster won two!

He won the Most Disobedient Dog in the Show, which just made Lyndz start laughing all over again. Then he won a rosette in Novelty section for walking on his hind legs. It's a pity there wasn't a rosette for the Dog Who Could Jump the Highest, because he'd probably have won that, too.

Emily won a red rosette with her cat and Emma Hughes won two. After Brown

The Pet Show

Owl had explained to the judges some of what had happened, and told them how perfect Snowball had looked when she arrived they gave her one rosette for being the Best Groomed Dog in the Show and then one for the Scruffiest Dog in the Show. All in the same afternoon.

Afterwards, we kept wondering when the trouble was going to land, but it never really did. Brown Owl wasn't so cross with us. Snowy Owl had seen how it had all started, so she knew it had been an accident. That was a lucky escape.

Rosie said Adam loved it when she told him the story of what happened out on the field. She had to keep telling him over and over. He was sorry he missed it.

When I told my mum all about it, she said we should try to keep away from the M&Ms for a while, so that's what we're doing. Anyway, since the Pet Show, they seem to be keeping away from us, too.

* * *

So that's the whole story. Come on, we're nearly home, just round this corner. Oh, look! Come on, quick. There's Pepsi, now, at my front gate. I'm so glad she's OK. She looks a bit mucky, though. I wonder who brought her back this time? Uh-oh, there's my mum at the door.

"Francesca, about time! I think you'd better come in and clean up this dog don't you?"

"Coming, Mum."

Oh, well, no rest for the wicked as my gran says. See you again soon. Bye.

The Sleepover Club at Felicity's

Join the Sleepover Club: Frankie, Kenny, Felicity, Rosie and Lyndsey, five girls who just want to have fun – but who always end up in mischief.

A sleepover isn't a sleepover without a midnight feast and when the food runs out and everyone's still hungry, the Sleepover Club tiptoe down to the kitchen. But – quick! – the toaster's on fire!

Pack up your sleepover kit and drop in on the fun!

0 00 675236 5